The Chocolate Lab

Lab

TUG-OF-WAR

EACH BOOK IS SWEETER THAN THE LAST!

The Chocolate Lab

TUG-OF-WAR

By **ERIC LUPER**

Scholastic Inc.

ISBN 978-0-545-90242-7

10 9 8 7 6 5 4 3 2 1   16 17 18 19 20

Printed in the U.S.A.   40

First printing 2016

Book design by Sharismar Rodriguez and Mary Claire Cruz

For Lily
(who keeps me super-excited
about chocolate)

Chapter 1

Without a Paddle

People always complain about the smell of wet dog. When something is damp and musty, people say, "Ew, it smells like wet dog around here!" They spray lemony spray in the air, burn candles that stink like pumpkin spice, and sprinkle baking soda all over the rug.

As for me, the smell of wet dog fills my nose with memories of summers in the creek behind our house. It reminds me of long walks in the rain with my chocolate Labrador retriever, Cocoa—my best buddy in the world. No, I think the smell of wet dog is the best, second only to the smell of melted chocolate.

The problem is that both of those smells—melted chocolate *and* wet dog—might be yanked right out of my life if Cocoa doesn't settle down and start behaving. My family is counting on rebuilding this old mill so we can make chocolate using an old Cabot family chocolate recipe. If Cocoa can't keep out of the way, we'll never save our candy business.

I bury my nose deep in Cocoa's fur and look at the pile of lumber he just knocked into the water. Then, I look up at Mr. Dave, the carpenter Grandpa Irving hired to restore the old mill.

The broken beams above us barely hold up the ceiling, which is filled with gaping holes. Garbage and dead leaves litter the floor. Out the door that faces the stream, a broken waterwheel hangs crookedly, like a sad emoji. I was the first to support Grandpa's ideas about restoring the mill, but now that I've actually been inside, I'm not so sure anyone should make chocolate in here . . . ever.

Several long pieces of lumber drift downstream.

"Cocoa's really sorry," I tell Mr. Dave, hugging Cocoa close. He drags his wet bologna tongue up my cheek. "One of your workers is drinking hot chocolate and the smell makes Cocoa go bananas."

"That dog . . ." Mr. Dave says, his cheeks burning bright pink. "That dog . . ."

Just then, Grandpa and Hannah march in. Grandpa is carrying a rolled-up parchment and a large cup of coffee. His beat-up tricorn hat sits crookedly on his head. Hannah looks worried.

"Mason, Dave, you won't believe what I found," Grandpa announces. He hands the cup to Mr. Dave.

"I prefer tea," Mr. Dave says.

"No builder of mine is going to support the Redcoats and their tea tax," Grandpa says. "Ever hear of the Boston Tea Party?" Grandpa isn't crazy. He's just crazy about Revolutionary War history. He likes to get together with his friends and reenact big battles from the war. It's kind of weird, but it makes him happy. And after Kunkle Kandies almost put our Towne Chocolate Shoppe out of business, Grandpa Irving helped us start selling our Great-Great-Great-Great-(however-many-times)-Grandma Beatrice's colonial chocolate recipe to his fellow reenactors. We call it Yankee Doodle Candy. And now we're going to try to make even more of it by turning the old mill into a chocolate factory.

Mr. Dave peels back the lid of his coffee and takes a sip. His face wrinkles behind his mustache, but he knows better than to argue with Grandpa.

Grandpa unrolls the parchment on the workbench and places tools on each corner to hold it open.

"What is it?" I ask.

Grandpa stands back. His round belly stretches the buttons of his shirt. "It's the original plans for this mill—straight from 1763. I found it in the basement at town hall. The stream is on the right. This should help us restore it to its original glory."

Hannah stands on her tiptoes so she can see.

I peer closely at the faded ink. The wavy lines look like water. I see a faint waterwheel and the rest of the mill. Little lines crisscross inside the building. It looks way more complicated than I imagined.

"You're not giving me a lot to go on," Mr. Dave says. "Plus, we already have the beams laid out in the opposite direction."

Grandpa smiles. "You'll figure it out."

But I'm not sure anyone could figure out all those crazy lines.

Hannah tugs on my sleeve and we head outside. A small bridge crosses the creek just upstream from us, where a dam holds the water back to a trickle. It doesn't look like there's enough water running past to turn a scooter wheel, let alone a giant waterwheel to grind big bags of cocoa beans.

"What's the matter?" I ask.

"I overheard Dad and Mom," Hannah says. "We're not selling enough Colonial chocolate in the shop, at the farmer's market, or at the local reenactments. If the mill isn't running by December first, we'll be out of money."

"But Grandpa said—"

"Grandpa is blinded by his love for this project," Hannah says. "He sold everything to make the mill work. The trouble is that restoring it costs way more than anyone imagined. We need to expand so we can make more chocolate and sell to more places."

I look down at the workers fishing the lumber out of the creek. Having Cocoa mess things up every day doesn't help. I grip his collar a little tighter.

"Then, we only have one choice," I say.

"What's that?" Hannah asks.

I tap the rough wood of the waterwheel. "We've got to get this thing turning in less than a month."

Chapter 2
A Cute Addition

Cars roll by behind us as Hannah and I sit at the top of the bridge. Our feet dangle toward the dam. Cocoa lies on the warm pavement, his head in my lap. The water behind the dam must be ten feet higher than the creek that trickles past our chocolate shop and the run-down mill across the way.

"People say if that dam wasn't here, most of our town would be a swamp."

"Actually, it would be a marsh," Hannah says.

"What's the difference?"

Hannah puts her chin on the railing that spans the bridge. "Swamps have woody plants. Marshes only have reeds and grass."

"How did—"

"Second-grade science."

"Did you learn how a Colonial-era chocolate mill works?" I ask.

Hannah squints over at me. "You took a field trip to Old Berkshire Village last year. Didn't you pay attention?"

"I was too mad. I wanted to go to the Baseball Hall of Fame."

Cocoa puffs through his nose.

"See? Cocoa would rather go to the Baseball Hall of Fame, too."

"You're both hopeless," Hannah says. "The water pushes the waterwheel until it starts spinning. That turns a bar that gets a bunch of belts and gears working. The belts turn a giant stone that's pressed up to another giant stone, which grinds whatever you put between them."

"In our case, cocoa beans," I offer.

"Exactly," Hannah says. "We won't have to use the mortar and pestle anymore. If we can find stones smooth enough, we won't have to use our tiny grinding stone, either."

"That would save us a ton of work," I say, thinking about Grandpa's ropy forearms working endless hours over the grinding stone.

"And we could make hundreds of pounds of chocolate a day instead of four or five," Hannah says. "We could make it for reenactments and historic sites all over the country."

But I barely hear that last part. The thought of a mill grinding that much chocolate distracts me. My mouth starts watering more than the stream below us.

Cocoa lifts his head and puffs through his

nose again. At first, I think he can read my thoughts, but I soon realize he's puffing about something else.

Cocoa's tags jingle against his collar as he stands up. He looks past our chocolate shop into the woods. He puffs again.

"What's wrong with your dog?" a shrill voice says.

It's Mrs. Kunkle, the owner of Kunkle Kandies, the chocolate shop on the other side of town. Even in the breeze, her superstrong perfume makes my eyes tear up. She's walking across the bridge with her son, Alan, and what looks like a bunch of pink cotton balls on a leash. Cocoa doesn't even glance at them.

"What's that?" Hannah says.

Mrs. Kunkle walks over. There's a dog under all that bright, poufy fur.

"This is Cotton Candy," Mrs. Kunkle says.

"C.C. for short," Alan adds. "She's our new poodle. And unlike your dog, she's perfectly trained."

"Cocoa is perfectly trained," I say.

"Ha," Alan says. "The only thing your dog is perfectly trained to do is destroy things."

My face gets hot.

"Oh, be nice, Alan," Mrs. Kunkle says.

Alan jiggles C.C.'s sparkly leash. "You've got a chocolate dog for your chocolate shop. Now we have a candy dog for our candy factory."

C.C. lifts her snout and says *hmpf*.

"Candy factory?" I say. "You have a blinkie machine in the front window of your store. I'd hardly call that a factory."

Alan scrolls through his phone with his free hand and turns it toward me. "Don't you read the business section? We just bought a building on the edge of town. We're moving there and starting delivery to Farm Fresh Foods. Kunkle Kandies is going global!"

"What do you know about going global?" Hannah says. "You barely passed history last year."

Alan narrows his eyes. "Just because I didn't do well in history doesn't mean I don't have other talents."

"Like what?" I say.

"Like science and engineering."

Cocoa looks more intently at the woods. He takes a few nervous dog steps and woofs softly.

"My Alan is a genius," Mrs. Kunkle boasts. "Show your friends the doodad you're working on."

Alan pulls something from his pocket. It's a tiny, green castle on a platform. "I'm making a chess set from scratch," Alan says. "Zombies versus Unicorns. I'm headed to the library now to make a queen."

"You can make a chess set at the library?" I try to hide my interest, but it's not easy.

"Sure," Alan says. "You just design it with the software and the new 3-D printer builds it for you."

He looks over the side of the bridge. "I also know enough about science to tell you this tiny creek won't have enough water to push that waterwheel. Before you even get started, Yankee Doodle Candy is going to be Yankee Doodle Closed-for-Business."

I want to tell Alan Kunkle that he has no idea what he's talking about, that this creek will power our mill so well we won't be able to keep up with all the chocolate pouring out of it.

But I look down at the sad trickle, and I'm afraid he's right.

Suddenly, Cocoa bolts for the woods.

Hannah and I chase after him. Alan's laughter and Mrs. Kunkle's perfume fade behind us. C.C. puffs a *hmph* in the distance.

Cocoa darts across a road. Cars screech to a stop. Horns honk.

I blurt an apology to Mrs. Pratt, our school music teacher, who's glaring at us from behind her steering wheel. I know I'll get a lecture from her on Monday, but right now I need to catch my dog.

Cocoa plunges into a cluster of bushes and starts rustling around.

By the time Hannah and I get there, we're out of breath. But before I have a chance to call for him, Cocoa marches back out.

A tiny yellow Lab puppy hangs from his mouth.

Chapter 3

Rotten Gear

"**What's** his name?"

"First of all, he's a *she*," Hannah says, looking at the dog's collar. "And her name's Nilla."

"What kind of name is Nilla?"

"It must be short for Vanilla."

The dog squirms in Hannah's arms. "I'm keeping her," she says.

"You can't just keep a dog you find on the side of the road."

"Sure I can," Hannah says. "We already

have a chocolate Lab named Cocoa. Nilla is the perfect addition."

"We can't even keep track of *one* dog," I say, giving Cocoa a scratch behind his ear. "Anyhow, Nilla has a collar, which someone put on her. Her owners are probably worried sick."

Hannah lowers her nose to Nilla's. Nilla's tongue darts out and licks Hannah's face. "Anyone who leaves a cute puppy like this on the side of the road doesn't deserve to own a pet in the first place."

I try to think of an argument, but it's hard. Nilla is so chubby and fluffy. And I can smell her puppy smell from here. "We've got the mill to worry about," I say.

"What can we do to help rebuild a Colonial-era mill, Mason? We're helpless."

I look across the river. The mill looks like a sagging pile of wet firewood. Mr. Dave's workers are pulling up planks so they can fix whatever mistake Grandpa said they made.

I spin Nilla's collar so I can read it. A long number is printed under her name. It reads:

10514141-M

"What's this?" I ask.

"Who knows?" Hannah says. "Maybe she escaped some mad scientist's laboratory and was waiting for a nice family like ours to adopt her."

"Someone out there must be missing her. We have to find her owners,"

Hannah thinks it over. "Okay, but if we can't, she's ours to keep."

"You're going to have to convince Mom and Dad of that."

• • •

"No way," Mom says as she rushes around the counter to straighten a display of purple, glittery chocolate boxes.

"But you didn't let me finish," Hannah pleads.

"You don't need to finish," Dad says from the back of the store. Even though we're not going to a reenactment anytime soon, he's wearing the Colonial clothing Grandpa got for him. His white shirt and blue vest are splattered with chocolate. "We already have a dog. He causes enough trouble as it is."

"Nilla won't be any trouble," Hannah says. "I promise!"

She scoots around the counter and hands

Dad a sheet of paper. "I made a flyer to help find her owner and everything."

Dad looks over the flyer. "We really should bring her to the dog shelter."

"Nilla can't go to doggie jail," Hannah says. "She's too young. The other dogs will be mean to her!"

"The dog shelter will know what to do," Mom says. "It's what they're good at. We're good at chocolate."

"What if she doesn't like it there?"

"She'll be fine," Dad says.

"What if no one comes to get her? What if another dog makes her sick? What if—"

Dad puts his hand on her shoulder. "Hannah, she'll be fine."

I watch as Nilla runs across the floor of the chocolate shop. She trips and falls right on her fluffy face. I smile, but I also wonder how another dog would fit into our family. For the longest time, it was just Mom, Dad, Hannah, and me. Then Cocoa came along and turned everything upside down. Having a second dog would mean double the feeding, double the walks, double the everything. My stomach knots up a little. I'm just not so sure it would work out.

Just then, Grandpa Irving charges into the store. "A wooden cogwheel! A ridiculous wooden cogwheel!"

My mother rushes over. "Irving, what's the matter?"

Grandpa throws his hands in the air. "One of the gears in the mill is rotted out. We need to have a new one made."

"Mr. Dave will figure it out," Dad says.

"He can't do it," Grandpa says. "If the wheel isn't exact, the mill won't turn. We have to bring in a master craftsman, and the only guy I know isn't available until springtime."

"This is getting more and more complicated," Mom says, wringing her hands in her apron.

"This is getting more and more expensive," Dad mutters.

Grandpa picks up a bar of our Colonial chocolate. "We're going to have to sell a lot more of these," he says. "Master craftsmen don't come cheap."

"Do you still have the old gear?" I ask.

"Sure," Grandpa Irving says, handing it to me. "But it's no use to anyone."

"Maybe I can figure something out."

Dad unbuttons his vest. "First, we have to figure out what to do with little Nilla."

The shelter parking lot is made of packed gravel, and I kick a few stones ahead of me. Even from outside the building, I can hear barking and yelping. I know they do important work here, but it still makes me sad to hear all those excited dogs.

Dad, Cocoa, and I lead the way from the car to the front door. Hannah lags behind, clutching Nilla in her arms.

The dog shelter itself looks like a bunch of small houses. I wonder if they do that on purpose, since these dogs don't have homes of their own.

As we enter, an electronic bell beeps. The smell of disinfectant stings my nose. The barking is way louder inside.

A woman in a blue fleece scurries around the counter. "Good morning, my dears," she says. "My name is Liza. How may I help you?"

Dad clears his throat. "My kids found a puppy. We were wondering what we should do with her."

Liza's eyes move to Cocoa. "I'd say that dog is around two or three years old. Not much of a puppy."

"No," Dad says. "Cocoa is along because he's nosy. Mason and Hannah found a yellow Lab on Park Avenue—behind the supermarket parking lot."

"Actually, Cocoa found her," I say.

"Her name's Nilla," Hannah adds.

"May I see her?"

A worker wearing a dog shelter sweatshirt swings open the door to the back room. The barking from the back gets louder.

Hannah jumps at the noise and backs away. "No!"

"Come on, my dear," Liza says. "I promise I won't bite."

Hannah walks over. Nilla lets out a yappy bark.

"A spirited one," Liza says.

"She's eighty percent cute and thirty percent smart," Hannah says. "She's only ten percent bark."

"That's a hundred and twenty percent," Liza says.

"She's a special dog," Hannah says.

"I can tell." Liza puts on her glasses and reads Nilla's collar. "Interesting serial number."

"We were wondering what that means," I say.

"It's a transport tag," Liza says. "Little Nilla was on her way from one place to another."

"Why would someone send a dog away from its home?" Hannah asks.

Liza puts Nilla on the floor and lets her toddle around. "Some places want certain kinds of dogs more than other places. So transport organizations try to get dogs where they're wanted most."

"And what happens to Nilla when we leave her with you?" Dad asks.

Liza holds out a treat for Nilla, who gobbles it down. She gives one to Cocoa, too. "We'll try to have the transport group come get her. Our vet will have a close look at her, and we'll make sure she's had all her shots."

Hannah glances nervously at the back room. "What if the transport organization doesn't want her?"

Liza smiles. "We'll try to find her a loving home around here. Who wouldn't want a cute puppy like Nilla? Now, I'll just need you to fill out a surrender form and we'll be all set."

Tears rush to Hannah's eyes and she scoops Nilla off the floor. "Surrender?" she cries. "Doesn't that mean give up?"

Dad looks at Hannah and Nilla. He leans in to Liza to talk quietly. "Do we have any other options?"

Liza thinks for a moment. "You could become a foster family."

"What's a foster family?" I ask.

"It means your family looks after Nilla until we find her a good home."

Hannah brightens. "Can we, Dad? Can we? Can we? Can we?"

Dad looks at Liza. He looks at the door to the back room. He looks at Hannah and Nilla. I think he's looking for a reason to say no.

"We *are* low on space here at the shelter," Liza says. "I wish we had some magical machine to make a new building with all new kennels in it. Or better yet, more homes willing to adopt."

A magical machine. The idea of a machine that can spit out new buildings, new kennels, or new homes gives me an idea. But the barking is so loud right now that I can't concentrate.

In fact, the barking is so loud that I think the building might already be overflowing with dogs. It's as though they're rooting for Nilla to come home with us.

Dad kneels in front of Hannah. "Do you promise to help look for her proper owners?"

Hannah nods.

"Do you promise to feed and walk her when she needs it?"

Hannah nods even harder. A smile starts spreading across her face.

"Do you promise to give her up when some-one comes to claim her?"

Even that gets Hannah's head bouncing up and down.

Dad sighs. "Your mother is going to kill me."

Chapter 5

3-D Problems

I find Alan at the big warehouse on the edge of town. A metal sign hanging over the door reads:

KUNKLE KANDIES
You know you want some.

He's sitting in a glass booth, watching giant machines burp out an endless parade of chocolates onto conveyor belts, when Cocoa and I show up. Robot arms swing back and forth, wrapping chocolates in red foil and stacking them neatly into boxes. C.C. sits quietly while Cocoa circles the room. He can smell the chocolate and it's driving him nuts.

"Why would I help you?" Alan says.

"Look, Alan, I know we don't really get along . . ."

"No, you were never nice to me."

"What? I—"

Alan leans forward in his chair. "Ever since I moved here, you've always narrowed your eyes at me. You've always ignored me."

I open my mouth to say something, but close it as I think back to the first time I met Alan.

"It was at recess two Septembers ago," I say. "You came to school with a box of chocolates from your parents' new shop."

"Exactly," Alan says. "And what did you do?"

I look down at the gear I brought for him to look at. It's the size of a dinner plate, but much thicker. "I told the lunch aide that the chocolates might have traces of nuts and that Lindsey Ling has a nut allergy."

"And what about two weeks later, when I brought in that watermelon carved to look like a shark for my birthday?"

I sag in my chair. "I told Mrs. Carter that we're not supposed to celebrate birthdays in class anymore."

"Do you think it's easy being the new kid in school?"

I shake my head. Cocoa stops pacing for a moment and presses his cold nose against my hand. "I didn't think—"

"Exactly," Alan says. "You didn't think."

Cocoa whines and starts circling the room again. He leaps up and puts his paws against the glass so he can see the chocolate better.

"I'm sorry," I say. "I didn't realize what I was doing."

"Do you know why I'm always texting on my phone?" Alan asks.

I shrug.

"I'm trying to stay connected with my friends back in New York City. The trouble is that they're all moving on. They're all forgetting about me."

My chest feels heavy and we both look down at the factory. Robotic arms tirelessly swing back and forth, wrapping mountains of chocolate. People wearing white poufy hairnets stack the boxes neatly while others load the cases onto trucks.

"At least you have all this," I say. "Farm Fresh Foods is a huge account."

Alan wipes the corner of his eye and scratches

C.C. behind her pink ear. "I'd trade it all for a halfway decent friend."

"What if we start with a little project?" I suggest.

Alan narrows his eyes at me. He doesn't trust me, and now that I think about it, I don't blame him.

"I'd owe you big-time," I say.

"You want a piece of chocolate?" he asks. "It doesn't have any nuts in it."

I laugh. "Sure."

Alan hands me a Kunkle Kandies Karamel Kluster. Strangely enough, I've never tried one of the Kunkles' chocolate bars. I tear off the wrapper and take a bite. It's better than I thought it would be. The chocolate melts over my tongue and seems to fill my whole mouth. The caramel comes next, a blast of more intense sweetness that gets my eyes rolling back. When I swallow it down, all I can think about is having more. I pop the rest in my mouth.

"I guess I don't need to ask what you think," Alan says. "Now, let me have a look at that gear."

I hand Alan the gear from the mill. Grandpa Irving wasn't kidding when he said it was useless. I practically poked my finger through the rotting wood, and several of the cogs are missing.

Alan spins in his chair and starts tapping away at his laptop.

"What are you going to do from your computer? I thought the 3-D printer was at the library."

Alan points to a table in the corner. A box that looks like a big toaster sits on top of it.

"The one at the library wasn't big enough to make parts for our machines, so I convinced my father to buy this one. It's just about the biggest one you can get."

"How does this work anyway?" I ask.

Alan points at the laptop. "I plot all the edges of whatever I want to print out, hit SEND, and watch the magic happen."

I look at the printer humming away. A metal jet zips around, laying down thin strands of green plastic, like icing on a tiny cake.

"What's it making?" I ask.

Alan lays the gear on his desk and starts looking at it from different angles. "A zombie pawn for my chess set," he says. "It takes awhile to print things out."

"How many pieces have you done?"

He motions to a small shelf. A few dozen chess pieces stand at attention. The green ones look like tiny zombies. The white ones look like little unicorns.

I take the tallest white one down. It's a unicorn king wearing a suit of armor and a crown around its horn. "These are nice," I say. "What about the chessboard?"

"I'm kind of stumped by that," Alan says. "Even this big printer isn't large enough to do a full-size board. Plus, some squares need to be green and others need to be white. My printer only does one color at a time."

I've never played chess, but I want to help Alan make his chess set. In some small way, I want to show him I'm sorry about the way I treated him. Anyhow, it sounds like a fun challenge to design all the pieces in the computer and see your ideas come out—kind of like getting new molds, pouring in melted chocolate, and seeing a chocolaty heart, bunny, or turkey pop out.

C.C. hops up next to Cocoa and they both look down at the factory. Their tails wag together like windshield wipers. I wonder why people don't make friends the way dogs do. They just seem to accept other dogs no matter what.

"Looks like C.C. and Cocoa are warming up to each other," I say, but Alan is in his own little world, completely focused on the gear in front of him. He puts it on a photocopier and scans it.

I think about Alan's chessboard. *Green squares and white squares. How would they all stay together?*

"Can you glue the plastic squares together?" I suggest.

"I tried that. It doesn't hold tight enough."

"What about melting them so the edges connect?"

"Too messy," Alan says.

Alan pulls out a ruler and measures the gear. "Same as the chessboard." He sighs. "Too big for the printer."

I look down at the chess piece in my hands. That unicorn king looks as though nothing worries him. He just stares off into the distance with all the confidence in the world.

I wish I felt like that.

But I don't. That heavy feeling in my chest just feels heavier.

Chapter 6

Cocoa seems immune to the chilly weather as he splashes along the stream near the mill. Nilla is happy following Cocoa back and forth, the two of them brown and yellow blurs. Mr. Dave asked us to keep the dogs away from the work site. He said it was a dangerous place for a pet, but I think that they were just getting in his way. Even Nilla was causing her share of trouble. She knocked over a big box of nails, which fell through the floorboards and into the mud.

"How's the hunt for Nilla's home?" I ask Hannah.

"I've got signs posted all over town, and Liza put her on the shelter website. Plus, we've traced the serial number on Nilla's collar to a pet rescue organization that sends dogs from Tennessee to the Northeast. It's named Fur-ever After Rescue and Transport. I called them and left a message."

"Did anyone call back?"

"It's only been a day," Hannah says. "Liza told me that rescue people are busier than long-tailed cats in a room full of rocking chairs."

Nilla is covered in mud, but that doesn't seem to bother her. She's grown on me, but the thought of keeping her stresses me out, too. Having one dog is a lot of work. Doubling that work seems too much to handle.

The mill is looking much better. The workers hauled away all the old wood. They have part of the frame built and are working on nailing down plywood so they can walk around. Another group of men are working on the guts of the mill, making sure the gears connect and that everything turns easily. A woman who always keeps a pencil behind her ear is replacing the paddles of the waterwheel. If they were building a person, they'd have part of the skeleton built.

I sigh. "Our problems seem to be getting bigger and bigger."

"What problems?" Hannah skips a stone across the stream. It bounces four times before disappearing with a splash.

I chuck a rock, but it just plunks into the water. "Finding a home for Nilla, getting the mill rebuilt, hoping the stream will be strong enough to turn the waterwheel, hoping Cocoa doesn't wreck everything."

"I don't worry about any of that stuff," Hannah says.

"How?"

"Things work out or they don't." She skips another stone. This one bounces five times. "If they don't, we'll figure out a way to fix them."

"But all these problems—"

"Mason, think of them as challenges, not problems. Remember when you and I had to win the Chocolate Expo? Did we just sit there and worry, or did we overcome each challenge?"

I squeeze the stone I'm holding. It warms in my fingers. "We worked our puppy-dog tails off," I say.

"Exactly," Hannah says. "That's what we need to do now."

"But there are so many more things to worry about."

"Then we have to work harder," Hannah says. "A problem drags you down. A challenge is asking to be solved. So, let's start solving."

"Where'd you learn all this stuff?" I ask her.

"A poster in Mrs. Pratt's room. It's of a kitten trying to do a puzzle."

"I've seen that poster," I say. "I've just never read the words."

"That's problem number one," Hannah says.

Grandpa Irving's pickup truck flies into the parking lot near the mill and skids to a stop. "Tongue and groove!" he hollers. "Tongue and groove!"

Hannah and I run over. Cocoa follows us. Nilla isn't far behind.

Mr. Dave puts down his saw and meets Grandpa by his truck. "What's going on?"

"Return the plank flooring we bought," Grandpa says. "If we want to stay true to the original plans, we need tongue-and-groove floorboards."

"How do you know?" Mr. Dave says.

Grandpa hands a piece of brown, flaky paper to Mr. Dave. "There was a supply list stuck to the back of the plans. It called for tongue-and-groove flooring."

"Tongue and groove sounds like a dance move," Hannah says. She sticks out her tongue and starts jumping around like a hip-hop performer.

Mr. Dave squints at the faded paper. "Tongue and groove is a type of joint between two pieces of wood. It's used when you're trying to connect two edges. One piece has a slot along it and the other has a ridge. When the ridge slides into the slot, it makes for a stronger connection, with no gaps."

Grandpa pulls two wood samples from the

back of his truck. He shows us how the boards fit together. "Airtight and strong," he says.

I take hold of it and feel along the edge. It feels like one solid piece of wood.

"So, all the flooring will fit together like this?" I ask.

"Like one big giant puzzle," Mr. Dave says.

And that gives me an idea. "Grandpa . . . Mr. Dave . . . Do you mind if I borrow this wood?"

Grandpa shrugs. "You can have 'em," he says. "They're just samples from the flooring store."

I tuck the planks under my arm and dart off.

"Where are you going?" Hannah calls after me.

"I'm overcoming a challenge!" I call back.

"Brilliant!" Alan says, looking closely at the two pieces of flooring. He spins in his chair and starts tapping at his computer. When he's done, he tilts the screen toward me.

"Each square on the chessboard gets printed out by itself—thirty-two green ones and thirty-two white ones," Alan continues. "If we're careful about how we do the ridges and the grooves, it should all fit together like a puzzle. This is really smart."

A warm feeling spreads through me. It feels

good to solve a problem. It also feels good to help someone else, especially a new friend.

I grab Cocoa's leash and stand up.

"Oh, you can't go yet," Alan says.

"Why not?"

Alan clicks his mouse a bunch of times and I look over his shoulder at the laptop. He's spinning the scan he made of my gear around on the screen.

"We can do the same thing with that gear you need." He unwraps a bite-size piece of Kunkle chocolate and pops it in his mouth.

Cocoa hears the wrapper and lifts his head. He sniffs a few times and puts his head between his paws. Even he seems to know how important this is.

"If we split the round gear into eight pie pieces and give each one a ridge and a groove, we can build the whole thing out of smaller pieces."

"Now *you're* the brilliant one," I say.

Alan smiles, but his gaze doesn't leave the monitor. His eyes look as eager as Cocoa's do when he watches Mom cooking meatloaf.

Before I know it, Alan has a pie piece on his screen. Three cogs stick out of the rounded edge. One straight edge has a ridge while the other has a groove. I can already see how it will all fit together.

"Your printer is big enough to make that?"

Alan squints at the screen. "Barely," he says. "But it'll take awhile."

"How long?" I ask.

"A few weeks," Alan says. "Nearly two days for each piece. They need to be strong enough to turn the crank without breaking. That's going to take a lot of plastic filament."

A few weeks puts us awfully close to when the mill needs to be working, but what choice do we have?

"Can you print out the picture of that pie piece for me?" I ask.

"Sure."

Within seconds, I'm holding a sheet of paper that shows Alan's tongue-and-groove gear piece from several angles.

I thank Alan, grab the printout and Cocoa's leash, and dart out the door.

. . .

"Who's ever heard of a plastic gear?" Grandpa says, shuffling past me into the mill. "Gears are made of iron. They're made of oak."

"What choice do we have?" I say. "We can't wait for your master craftsman in the spring, and we have no other way of making a gear."

Mr. Dave takes the printout from me. He looks closely at the image. "You say you can spit this out of a printer?" he asks.

"It's a special kind of printer," I say. "But yeah . . ."

"And your friend says it'll only cost fifty bucks in plastic filament to make it?"

"It's got to be cheaper than bringing in a master craftsman," I say.

Mr. Dave shakes his head in disbelief. "Irving, I don't see that we have a choice. Let's give the kid a shot."

Grandpa Irving smiles. "Mason is as much a part of this project as anyone. If he says this gear will work, then it'll work."

"Nilla, come back here!" It's Hannah. She's got Cocoa on a leash, but Nilla is running around on the lawn between the mill and the parking lot. Nilla's grown a lot in the few weeks since we found her. Her legs are longer and she isn't tripping onto her face as much.

"What are you doing?" I ask Hannah.

"I'm training Nilla. Mom and Dad won't be able to say no to adopting her if she behaves like an angel. I mean, they put up with Cocoa and he's a crazy tornado."

A pang of jealousy strums through me. What if Nilla steals my parents' love? What if they start liking her better than they like Cocoa? Having an angel around the house might be terrible for my dog.

Hannah grabs Nilla by the collar and sits her down. She takes a few steps back. "Stay," Hannah says. Nilla stays. "I watch a show called *Doggie Daycare with Diego Mirón.*"

"You learned how to train dogs on television?"

"And YouTube videos. The most important part is to let the dog know I'm the alpha."

"What's an alpha?"

"It means I'm the boss. Once she knows that, it's all about positive reinforcement. Praise her when she does something right." Nilla is still sitting quietly.

"Good girl!" Hannah says. Nilla jumps up and snatches a treat from Hannah. "I've already taught her sit and stay. Next comes lie down. She's a quick learner."

Cocoa is looking out over the stream at our chocolate shop and straining against his collar. The breeze is carrying the scent of roasting cocoa beans across to us. Mom likes to roast the beans on Saturday. The scent brings in tons of customers.

Suddenly, Cocoa leaps forward. The leash slips from Hannah's fingers, and Cocoa darts across the lawn. He takes a huge jump from the shore, splashes into the water, and starts paddling.

"Any chance you can help Cocoa learn who's the alpha?"

Hannah shakes her head. "I'm not sure that dog will ever learn anything."

Chapter 8

Another Doggie Disaster

It takes me a few minutes to run up the street and across the bridge. By the time I get to the shop, Cocoa has done his damage. The floor is soaked with stream water. The display of purple boxes Mom had been working on is knocked down; trays of Chocolate Peanut Butter Bumps are dumped on the floor; and a batch of newly made, warm, gooey chocolate is dripping down the side of the workbench.

The incredible scent of roasting cocoa beans does distract me a little. It lights up a deep, deep part of my brain and makes me feel relaxed. It doesn't seem to have that same effect on my parents.

"Mason, get Cocoa out of here!" Mom hollers. "That dog is incorrigible!"

"What does *incorrigible* mean?" I ask, out of breath.

My father grabs my shoulders and looks me in the eyes. His face is pink and he's breathing even harder than I am. "It means he can't be cured. How many times have we told you to keep that dog on his leash?"

"He *is* on a lea—"

"Then how did he get in here?" Mom snaps, beginning to stack the purple boxes back on the front counter.

"I'm sorry," Hannah says, standing in the open doorway. Nilla sits quietly at her feet. "I was holding the leash. He got away from me."

That seems to cool Mom and Dad off a little. Their fury lessens when my organized, responsible sister does something wrong.

"Please get Cocoa into his crate while we clean up," Mom says. "We have enough problems as it is without that dog wrecking everything."

Tears swell in my eyes, but I choke them back down. I grab Cocoa's wet leash and lead him to his crate. I make sure the latch is locked tight and head back to the shop to help clean up.

I mop the floor extra well while Mom rearranges the displays. Dad keeps an eye on the roasting cocoa beans while he sponges off the workbench. Hannah wipes down the glass of the display case.

"Any word on Fur-ever After Rescue and Transport?" Dad asks Hannah as he jiggles the cast-iron roasting pan a few times.

Hannah pauses before she answers. "The woman's name is Cindi Shaw. I spoke to her yesterday. She comes through town the last Saturday of every month, but she's delayed a week because of Thanksgiving."

"That's the grand opening of the chocolate mill," Dad says.

I look out the back window of the shop. The waterwheel is still hanging crookedly, and the roof is covered with blue plastic. Even though Grandpa Irving and Mr. Dave insist that the mill will be finished in time, I can't help but worry.

"Just have Ms. Shaw come to the grand opening," I suggest.

Mom's tower of purple boxes is almost done. "Just what we need, another distraction."

"Nilla is *not* a distraction," Hannah barks.

Mom comes around the counter. "I'm sorry.

Nilla isn't a distraction. We're just a little stressed out with everything going on."

Hannah purses her lips and goes back to wiping the glass.

Dad turns off the stove, jiggles the cast-iron pan one last time, and brings a plate to the front of the store. "Now, what are we going to do with these four Chocolate Peanut Butter Bumps that landed on the counter?" he asks.

"Looks like there's one for each of us," Mom says.

I snatch mine without a pause and shove the whole thing in my mouth. The scent of the roasting cocoa beans only makes the chocolate taste better. My mouth floods with the smooth taste of homemade chocolate, followed by the sharp, salty bite of the peanut butter. My breath cuts a little short and my eyes roll back.

Hannah grabs hers and takes a tiny bite. Her scowl turns into a smile.

Dad messes her hair, grabs his chocolate, and goes back to work.

"Ms. Shaw is more than welcome to come to our grand opening," Mom says. "Maybe we'll even cook up a little surprise for those lucky puppies she's bringing up north."

Hannah's smile widens and she eats the rest of her chocolate.

Mom eats hers, and soon we're all happy again. Chocolate sort of does that for our family.

Chapter 9

Eight Slices

A few weeks later, we're all checking out how the mill is coming along, when Mr. Dave pops his head up from a hatch in the floorboards. "Everything is looking great. Any idea when the gear will be finished?"

"I spoke to Alan earlier," I say, looking down from a new balcony in the rafters. "He said it should be done today."

"Doesn't give us much room for error," Grandpa says. "The grand opening is on Saturday. The mayor is coming to cut the ribbon."

Saturday. That's five days away. My chest flutters and my palms get sweaty. There's no way this place will be ready in five days.

Grandpa puts a reassuring hand on my shoulder.

"Why do they cut a ribbon when they open a new business?" Hannah asks. She's sitting with Cocoa and Nilla by a railing that faces the stream. It's a chilly day and her scarf is wrapped so high around her head that I can barely see her face.

Grandpa Irving stares across the stream. "I don't rightly know when it started, but it means a new beginning, like whatever is behind that ribbon is ready and waiting to be shared with the world."

"Hopefully they bring fistfuls of money," I say.

Alan stomps through the door holding a

tote bag. C.C. follows close behind. Her fur is lime green today. She rushes over to Nilla and Cocoa out on the porch.

Alan taps something into his phone and reads from the screen. "The ribbon-cutting ceremony was first done in 1898 to open a railroad in Louisiana. But ribbon cutting has been done in other cultures for centuries, mostly for weddings."

"That little box told you that?" Grandpa asks him.

"Amazing what this little box can do."

Grandpa waggles his head. "What happened to the days of good old-fashioned conversation?"

"It disappeared with the days of not knowing stuff," Alan mumbles.

I rush over to Alan. "Do you have the pieces for the gear?"

Alan hands his tote bag to Mr. Dave. "Hot off the printer," he says.

Mr. Dave pulls out one of the pieces. It's bright orange and as big as a wedge of cheese. He pulls out a purple one and slides the two together to make a quarter circle. "Clever," he says.

Alan beams. "I didn't have enough plastic filament to do the whole gear one color. When it's all together, it kind of looks like a pinwheel."

Grandpa moves closer and peers down his nose at the pieces lying on Mr. Dave's work-bench. "How're you going to make them stick together," he asks. "That gear has to be strong enough to turn a grindstone."

"It's the strongest plastic available for a 3-D printer," Alan says. "Not sure about the glue."

"We can use epoxy resin," Mr. Dave says. "It'll be stronger than steel."

"And it only takes five minutes to harden," Grandpa adds.

Mr. Dave laughs. "So, you *do* know something about the twenty-first century, Irving."

"A few things . . ."

Before long, we're all wearing blue rubber gloves. Grandpa, Hannah, Alan, and I are holding two wedges each, and Mr. Dave is mixing together two gooey liquids in a cup with a Popsicle stick.

"Once the epoxy is on, we'll only have a few minutes to make sure all the pieces are tight and lined up perfectly." He raises the Popsicle stick and the gooey liquid drips down in a long, glistening string. "Are you ready?"

We all hold up our wedges.

Mr. Dave drips the epoxy onto the ridges

and into the grooves. When they're all coated, we stand in a circle and fit our eight wedges together, like sliding eight slices of pizza into the shape of a circle. In a few minutes, Mr. Dave has the whole thing wrapped tightly with a strap to dry.

"We'll let this sit for a few days before mounting it to the axle under the mill," Mr. Dave says. "By then, my workers should be done with the waterwheel, and we'll be ready to give everything a test spin."

"You mean the mill will actually work?" Hannah asks excitedly.

Mr. Dave kneels down in front of Hannah. "It'll work if that gear holds up."

"And if it rains soon," Grandpa says, looking out the window. "Not sure there's enough water in that stream to make a pot of coffee."

．．．

The next few days I barely sleep. I worry about what we'll do if the waterwheel won't turn. I worry about Cocoa wrecking the grand opening, and whether we'll be able to sell enough chocolate to save our business. The sign isn't even up. How are people supposed to know where to go? Mom tells me those are problems for the grown-ups to worry about, but I can't help it.

I get up in the morning, go to school, and trudge around all day in a nervous fog. To clear my mind, I decide to read on the porch of the chocolate shop, but the words get all jumbled up in my head.

"Want to help me train Cocoa?" Hannah asks me from the lawn.

Nilla is sitting quietly while Cocoa paces near the fence.

"Um, sure," I say, tossing my book on the porch swing. "What do I do?"

"Cocoa already knows how to sit and stay," Hannah explains. "We just need him to know how to do that even when he smells chocolate. I've been working with him and he's gotten a lot better, but when the scent gets strong he loses control."

"Who doesn't?"

Hannah and I take turns holding Cocoa by the collar and keeping him calm while the other walks around the yard waving mom's Chocolate Marshmallow Fluff Puffs and Salted Caramel Graham Cracker Melts. He's definitely getting better at it, but even I can't sit still when they get too close.

Nilla stays where she is. Her head tilts a little when she sees Cocoa start getting excited. Cocoa pulls forward and whines. His tongue darts out to lick his nose.

I pet Cocoa lightly on his shoulder and whisper for him to stay. It's the first time in days I've felt relaxed.

Hannah gets closer.

Before long, Cocoa tears away from me, takes a few mad laps around the yard, and leaps over the fence. By the time I get out to the sidewalk, Cocoa's tail has disappeared around the house. The next I see of him, he's splashing in the stream and nipping at the water droplets in the air.

Hannah sighs loudly. "That dog . . ."

I want to run and play with Cocoa, but I worry about what will happen if Cocoa decides to behave like this during the grand opening. I can see it now—Grandpa falling into the freezing water, Cocoa tearing boards off of the waterwheel, and some local photographer snapping pictures that will end up on the front page of the local newspaper. If anything is going to ruin opening day, it'll be my dog.

Chapter 10

It's a chilly morning, one of the first where there's frost on the tips of the grass. The sky glows pink. Mist hangs low over the stream.

We're all holding our breath.

Everyone agreed to meet before school to see if the waterwheel turns. Grandpa said he'd hate to cut that ribbon with the mayor if the gear wasn't going to work. But he wanted to try it out secretly so we don't ruin the surprise on Saturday.

With two days left until the big event, I'm not sure what we'll do if it's a bust.

So here we are—me, Hannah, Grandpa, Mom, Dad, and Mr. Dave—under a dim light-bulb dangling from one of the rafters. Grandpa's hand is on the lever that sends the stream water down a channel that should turn the water-wheel. Mr. Dave cut a hole in the wall and fitted it with glass so we could watch Alan's rainbow-colored gear. I worry that it will burst apart with the mill's first turn.

"Everyone ready?" Grandpa asks.

I clench my fists into balls.

Dad squeezes Mom's hand.

Hannah starts shifting from foot to foot.

Mr. Dave takes a sip of his tea. "As ready as we'll ever be, Irving."

Grandpa pulls the lever. A chain jingles. Something thunks behind the wall. I hear the sound of trickling water. Hannah and I run out onto the dock. The waterwheel stands like a gray giant. Water rushes down the channel and starts splashing against the lowest paddles.

The waterwheel squeaks.

It moves slightly. Then it stops.

The water tumbles past, but the wheel doesn't turn.

Grandpa pulls the lever harder. It doesn't help.

Mom buries her face in Dad's sweatshirt. Mr. Dave puffs through his nose.

"What does this mean?" I say.

Grandpa looks down at the water trickling past the motionless waterwheel. "It means we think of a solution."

"Kids, come on," Mom says. "You have to get to school." She grabs our hands and begins to lead us out of the mill.

Hannah doesn't budge. Her hand slips from

Mom's grasp. She pulls a crumpled piece of paper from her pocket and hands it to Mr. Dave.

Mr. Dave squints at the paper and looks out the window toward the bridge.

I try to peek, but Mr. Dave is already on the dock taking measurements. His eyes shift between the bridge and the waterwheel.

Mom takes Hannah's hand more firmly. "Let's go, baby."

"Can you do it?" Hannah asks Mr. Dave.

His head nods slightly. "I reckon it's our best shot."

• • •

By the time we get home from school, Mr. Dave's team is building some sort of wooden chute that leads from the top of the dam to the waterwheel. Mr. Dave is working on a lever next to the one that Grandpa Irving pulled earlier this morning.

Grandpa rushes in. "I spoke to the mayor. She says we can finish the project, but we'll have to apply for a permit at the next town board meeting."

"Good," Mr. Dave says. "This idea of Hannah's may be the only thing that'll save the mill."

"That granddaughter of mine sure is a smarty-pants," Grandpa agrees. "I wonder how she figured out that we needed an overshot waterwheel instead of an undershot one."

I figured Hannah would be here after school, but she's across the river at the chocolate shop. She's in the front yard spending time with Cocoa and Nilla. It surprises me how much effort she's putting into those dogs.

But when I look at them, both Cocoa and Nilla are sitting quietly as Hannah marches around the yard with what looks like a Dark Chocolate Praline Melt-away. Cocoa twitches excitedly, but he keeps his bottom on the ground. Nilla lies down.

"What's an overshot waterwheel?" I ask.

Mr. Dave pulls a screwdriver from his tool belt and begins tightening a bracket onto a post. "Some waterwheels are pushed by a stream that goes underneath it. Those are called *undershot* waterwheels. Others have water tumbling down onto the paddles from above. Those ones are called *overshot*."

Grandpa is stacking a bunch of old-fashioned crates next to a barrel. He's working hard to make this old mill look *really* old. "Overshot waterwheels are much stronger than undershot ones. We should have that grindstone turning easy!"

"Sounds great," I say. "When will we get a chance to test it?"

"We won't," Mr. Dave says. "We'll be building this sucker right up until Saturday morning."

My breath cuts short. "What happens if the waterwheel doesn't turn in front of Mom and Dad, the mayor, the local paper, and all the rest of the people who show up to try our Yankee Doodle Candy?"

Grandpa straightens up and stretches his back to both sides. "Then we gave it our best shot, kiddo."

My face reddens just thinking about it—all of us standing there next to the waterwheel with everyone watching. Grandpa pulls the lever. The waterwheel looks down and laughs at us.

Then everyone else joins in. We'd be the joke of the town.

"I'm not sure—"

Grandpa takes me by the shoulders and looks me right in the eyes. "Mason, being fearless is having fears, but jumping anyway."

"Who said that?" I say. "Ben Franklin or Thomas Jefferson or some other ancient dude?"

Grandpa smiles. "Actually, it was Taylor Swift."

"I don't like Taylor Swift. She wears too much lipstick."

"Whether or not you like her lipstick doesn't mean she doesn't have something important to say. Now, give us some space to work. Your sister needs your help."

Chapter 11

Shifting Gears

The next afternoon, I jump off the porch onto the front lawn and hand the phone to Hannah. She's in the yard with the dogs. Cocoa is sniffing around the fence while Nilla is sitting on her hind legs waiting for a treat.

Hannah puts the phone to her ear and starts nodding her head. "Uh-huh . . . Okay . . . On Saturday . . . Yes, in the morning . . . 10 am . . ."

Hannah clicks off the phone and her cheeks turn red. She looks down at Nilla.

I sit down next to Cocoa and rub his belly. "What's the matter?"

"That was Liza from the shelter," Hannah explains. "She said Ms. Shaw, the transport lady, will be coming through town on Saturday morning with a carload of puppies. She's planning to be at the grand opening to pick up Nilla and continue north to New Hampshire."

"That's great!" I say. "Nilla will end up where she's supposed to be."

"She's supposed to be with us!" Hannah hollers and storms off.

I sit on the porch and both dogs come over. Cocoa lies down and rests his head on my lap, while Nilla hops up and tries to lick my face. I let Nilla's tongue reach my cheek. Her tail starts wagging harder than before. I know I was looking forward to Nilla finding her way back to her transport, but now I'm not sure.

Across the river, construction is going well. Crisscrossing beams hold up a chute that runs from the top of the dam and slopes toward the mill. It looks ready to dump tons of water on the waterwheel. I can already smell all of the thick Colonial-style chocolate we'll be making soon.

Or maybe that's the smell from the shop behind me. Mom and Dad have barely come out these last few weeks. They've been roasting cocoa beans nonstop so we'll have enough to grind on Saturday. Plus, they want to make sure we've got enough finished chocolate to sell. The local TV station has already done a story on the event, and we spent our last few dollars on ads in the paper. As for me, I've stapled posters to every telephone pole in town.

"Smells good," Alan says from the sidewalk. C.C. is with him.

I nod.

Alan comes inside the fence and sits beside me. The three dogs sniff one another and start wrestling over a stick.

"You know what I like to do when I get stressed out?"

"I'm not stressed out," I say.

"Of course you are. You've got a lot going on."

Alan unzips his backpack and pulls out a velvet pouch. He opens it and dumps a bunch of chess pieces on the porch, half green, half white.

I pick up a green queen and look closely at her. Zombie hands lurch out in front of her. Stringy hair tumbles out from beneath a tilted crown. A crooked smile makes her look fierce. "These are amazing."

"Thanks," Alan says, "But that's not the best part."

He pulls out a large green-and-white chessboard. The joints match up perfectly. I try to bend it, but it stays rigid, as though it's one solid piece of plastic.

"This is even more amazing," I say.

"It was your idea," Alan says, laying the board between us on the porch. He begins to set up the pieces.

"I don't know how to play," I admit.

"It's easy," Alan says.

"Chess is *not* easy."

"Okay," he says, making sure all the pieces are facing forward. "It's easy to learn, but hard to become good."

"A lot of things are like that," I say.

Alan shrugs.

I look at the chess pieces all lined up, working as a team. I think of Hannah, Grandpa Irving, Mom, Dad, and me. Mr. Dave is part of our team, too. Even Alan joined us. And that feels good. I hate to admit it, but, lipstick or not, Taylor Swift might be right. It's okay to have fears, but that doesn't mean you shouldn't push forward anyway.

Just like Hannah's been doing with Nilla. My sister's been on our chocolate mill team all along, but who's been on her dog rescue team?

I pick up the chess pieces and toss them back into the velvet pouch.

"We haven't even started yet," Alan says.

"Another time. How'd you like to help me train a couple of dogs?"

"Train dogs? That's what obedience school

is for. C.C. is going to Madame Beatrice's Finishing Academy for the Canine Elite."

"Is that where she learned to prance at the end of her glittery leash and say *hmph* at me?"

"She doesn't say *hmph*!" Alan says defensively, but I can tell from his smile that he knows she does. "Okay," he says, sliding the chessboard back into his backpack. "Let's train some dogs."

Chapter 12

Ribbon Time!

The morning of the grand opening is surprisingly warm, and the sun makes everything sparkle. Most everyone from town has come out. They're all crowding in front of the brand-new Yankee Doodle Candy Chocolate Mill. Even the high-school band is here playing patriotic tunes.

Grandpa, Mom, Dad, Hannah, and I are all wearing our Colonial clothing. Mayor Bartley stands with my parents behind a red ribbon that stretches across the door. Dad is holding a giant pair of golden scissors. Grandpa chats with Mrs. McEneny from the farmer's market, and Hannah plays with the dogs on the lawn. Liza from the shelter keeps looking at her watch and glancing up the road. Alan is here with C.C., whose fur has been dyed blue with red and white stripes.

"I know I'm supposed to be excited," Hannah says, "but I can't stop thinking about that lady coming to take Nilla away."

"Ms. Shaw is doing an important job," I say. "Don't be angry with her."

Hannah exhales. "I know, but everyone has been so focused on the mill that nobody's given much thought to what's best for Nilla . . . or what's best for me."

I put my arm around Hannah's shoulders and look over at Dad. He knows what we're talking about and he shakes his head no.

We walk over to him. "But, Dad," I say. "Hannah's been working really hard with Nilla. And Alan and I stayed up extra late to practice with both dogs. We're teaching them to get out their stress by running instead of destroying things. They've both come a long way."

"I told you before. We can't take on another dog," Dad says. "We're too busy to give her the attention she needs."

"Mason and I will do it," Hannah pleads. "You won't have to worry about a thing."

"I don't know, Hannah," Mom says. "Giving her up was part of our agreement, remember? She's a foster puppy. You have to learn to say good-bye to foster puppies."

Just then, a red station wagon pulls up and a shorthaired woman gets out. Her fleece reads: FUR-EVER AFTER RESCUE AND TRANSPORT. She opens the hatchback, and the sound of barking joins the music of the band. The back of her car is lined with cages, each one holding a different dog. The cage in the middle is empty, waiting for Nilla.

Tears rush to Hannah's eyes. "I'd better get to saying good-bye then."

Ms. Shaw comes down from the parking lot. "There's little Nilla," she says. "She must have slipped away when I stopped to walk them. She's grown so much!"

I smirk. "You know, if you put the first letters of your organization's name together it spells—"

"I know," Ms. Shaw says, looking at her fleece. "We didn't realize until after we had the shirts printed up."

"Can you give Hannah a few last minutes with Nilla?"

"Sure," she says. "The next leg of the transport meets at noon in Bennington."

"So you only drive part of the way?" I ask.

Ms. Shaw nods. "We share the journey so no one has to travel too far."

The band stops. Mom and Dad wave for us to join them with Mayor Bartley near the ribbon. After the Mayor says some stuff about the growth of the town and economic development, she hands the microphone to Dad.

Dad's face flushes and he says, "I'm not very good at speeches. Why don't we let the real brains behind this project speak?"

I turn to watch my father hand the microphone to Grandpa, but he hands it to me.

"I didn't write a speech," I say.

"Just speak from your heart," Mom says.

Speak from the heart. Speak from the heart.

I take a deep breath and let it out. "My . . .

uh . . . My heart doesn't have a lot to say right now."

The crowd chuckles.

I look at Grandpa. He's smiling bigger than ever.

Alan and C.C. are standing at the front of the crowd. Alan is smiling, too.

Even Hannah has taken her nose out of Nilla's fur to listen.

"We're very excited for the grand opening of our Yankee Doodle Candy Chocolate Mill. Thank you all for coming today."

Everyone claps. When it dies down, I go on.

"This project took hard work from a lot of different people. My grandpa Irving did the research to make the renovation true to the original building. Mr. Dave and his team built it. Then there's Mom and Dad, who have been making chocolate for this event. I hear they have a few new recipes, so be sure to buy some after we cut the ribbon."

The crowd laughs some more.

"And then, there's my sister, Hannah, who found a passion of her own. But she still took time away from her foster puppy to help out."

Hannah smiles and gives me a thumbs-up.

"But sometimes you find help where you least expect it. Big thanks to Alan Kunkle of Kunkle Kandies for designing and building an important gear for this mill. Keep your eyes open for the one that looks like a rainbow pinwheel. And be sure to try some Kunkle Kandies. They do a pretty good job over there, too."

I see Mr. and Mrs. Kunkle at the back of the crowd. They both wave.

"Fear is a strange thing," I say. "Some kids are afraid of the dark. Others are afraid of scary movies. I was afraid of taking on a big project when I knew I might fail. Fear can be important because it warns us when something might be dangerous. But if we worry about stuff that hasn't happened yet—things in the future—we let fear stop us from doing what we need to do here in the present . . . and that's bad. If my family had given in to fear, we might not have our candy store anymore, and we definitely wouldn't have this new mill."

I smile at Grandpa, who is nodding his head.

I turn back to the crowd. "So, I guess what I'm saying is, don't let fear stop you from going after what you want. Now, everyone enjoy some chocolate today. Let's cut that ribbon and get the waterwheel turning!"

Dad holds up the giant golden scissors. Mom, Dad, Grandpa, and I grab the handles. Hannah leaves Nilla to hold on. I wave over Mr. Dave and Alan, and we cut.

The ribbon floats to the ground and everyone cheers louder than ever. The band starts playing again, and everyone crowds closer to the mill. They're all dying to try some chocolate.

Grandpa takes the first lever and pulls it. Water runs under the waterwheel and rushes around the paddles. The wheel budges a little, but it doesn't turn.

Grandpa pulls the second lever. A chain goes tight and lifts a barrier at the top of the chute near the dam. Water flows down and splashes over the paddles on the waterwheel. I hold my breath.

The wheel begins to move. It turns halfway around, and then squeaks to a halt.

This is the moment I've been worried about.

Dad wraps his arm around Mom.

Grandpa turns away. "I was afraid that might happen," he mutters.

Chapter 13

The Dogs' Turn

The band stops playing.

"What does this mean?" Hannah asks.

"Give me three weeks," Mr. Dave says. "We'll build a new channel and get more water to pour down over that waterwheel."

"We don't have three weeks," Mom says. "We needed this waterwheel to work today."

Just then, Hannah cries out, "Cocoa, come back!"

Cocoa shoots between my feet and runs past Grandpa. He jumps onto one of the waterwheel's paddles and starts running up them one at a time.

The wheel budges.

Cocoa keeps running. Every time he reaches as high as he can go, the wheel turns a little more.

"It's like a giant hamster wheel," I say.

"He's so close," Mayor Bartley adds.

Suddenly, Nilla darts away from Hannah. She jumps down next to Cocoa and starts running up the inside of the waterwheel as fast as she can with her little paws.

The waterwheel turns some more.

And some more.

Before long, the waterwheel is turning freely and the dogs trot along with big doggie smiles on their faces. The wheel makes a thumping sound as it spins. Cocoa and Nilla hop out, and the wheel keeps turning on its own.

Grandpa laughs. "It's the world's only puppy-powered waterwheel!"

Hannah and I run inside and look at the rainbow gear. It's doing its job perfectly.

Grandpa dumps a sack of roasted cocoa beans on the grindstone, and it crushes them into a thick paste.

The crowd cheers. The band starts playing again. Mom and Dad give each other a hug. They pull us over and hug us, too. Grandpa puts his arms around us all.

The crowd rushes in and starts buying chocolate. Grandpa works the grindstone, which can crush as many cocoa beans as we can pour in. Dad works the cash register, which is soon overflowing with money.

Mom sits between Hannah and me on the edge of the dock. Cocoa is under my arm. Nilla is under Hannah's. The waterwheel churns behind us.

"You two make me so proud," Mom says, a happy tear rolling down her cheek. "Your father and I have been so busy these past few weeks that we've barely had a chance to talk. Both of you took on this challenge like grown-ups and look how it all turned out."

Hannah and I both lean into Mom. She puts her arms around us.

"It looks like you've got some great little workers there." It's Ms. Shaw.

"Thanks," Mom says. "Mason and Hannah have really–"

"Actually, I was talking about Cocoa and Nilla," Ms. Shaw says. "That waterwheel wouldn't be turning without them. Looks like you'll be keeping her, huh?"

Mom's mouth opens, then closes.

Finally, Mom nods.

Hannah squeals and hugs Nilla, who starts licking Hannah's face and wagging her tail.

Ms. Shaw winks at me. "But you know there are strict labor laws for animals in this state. You can't have those dogs working all the time."

"Oh, I'm sure we'll have this all figured out soon," Mom says.

Ms. Shaw kneels beside us. She's got another puppy snuggled against her chest. The puppy peeks out at us. It's a tiny black Lab. He's wearing a plastic collar with a serial number printed on it.

"His name is Licorice," Ms. Shaw says. "He'd be a great addition to your candy-making team."

Hannah squeals louder. "Can we, Mom? Can we? Can we? Can we?"

Mom laughs. "Every time we bring another dog into our family, something amazing happens. And you two have done a really great job training these two."

"That means we can keep him?" I say.

Mom glances at Dad, who's smiling at the three dogs scrambling all over us, and then shrugs. "Why not?"

Ms. Shaw hands Licorice to Mom and he yaps. Then he curls up and goes to sleep in her lap.

"Not much of a worker," Mom jokes.

Mom hands Ms. Shaw a paper bag. "Treats for your puppies," she says. "I baked them myself. One hundred percent chocolate-free."

"They'll love these," Ms. Shaw says. "Thanks!"

"Stop by anytime you come through town. I'll have a bag waiting for you."

Ms. Shaw smiles. "I'll get the release paper-work for Nilla and Licorice together."

I walk along the dock and let the breeze cool me.

I think back on how I felt when Hannah first found Nilla in the weeds. I was afraid bringing another pet into our house would split the love that we gave to Cocoa. I look at Grandpa and Dad working in the store. I look at Alan and Hannah playing with Cocoa, Nilla, C.C., and Licorice on the lawn. I look at every-one else in town having a great time at our brand-new chocolate mill. It's just now that I realize one thing: You can't split love, you can only multiply it.

Then I run out onto the front lawn and join the fun.

Chapter 1

You've got to be nuts if you don't like dog snuggles. There's nothing better than waking up late on a Saturday morning with a warm, fluffy dog sleeping right beside you. I love when that dog lifts its head and then drops it back down, happy to be lying in your comfy bed, too.

Sure, sometimes the dog stretches and pushes you over the edge. Sometimes you wake up to find your face squashed against your dog's rear end. But dog snuggles are the best.

The trouble is that I never get to wake up next to a dog because our Labradors never let me get to sleep in the first place. Our chocolate Lab, Cocoa, has always vibrated with energy. And ever since we adopted Nilla, our yellow Lab, and Licorice, our black Lab, all three dogs have decided they like camping out with me.

That's why I'm so tired while pushing the broom around the old mill my family runs to make our authentic Colonial-era chocolates. The waterwheel turns. The gears clink, clink, clink. And I push my broom slower than a zombie wading in caramel.

"You missed the corners, kiddo," Grandpa says as I bump into his feet.

"Sorry," I grumble.

I know it doesn't sound like it, but the past few months at the mill have been great.

Grandpa Irving makes chocolate the way

we learned to do it from my great-great-great-great-(however many times) grandmother's cookbook, which we found behind one of the walls of our house.

Dad works in the store, which has been busy, busy, busy, with people who can't resist buying our melt-in-your-mouth chocolate.

Mom is the food artist. She takes Grandpa's big bricks of chocolate and turns them into her famous bite-size candies. She grabs a bunch of ingredients you'd never think of putting together and creates something that makes you think you've skipped the dying part and gone straight to heaven.

As for my sister, Hannah, she's too busy to spend much time in the shop since she's gotten involved in animal rescue. She sets up rides for dogs that need to find forever homes. Every Saturday, she meets Ms. Shaw's van to help walk the dogs and give them water. She also brings along a bag of treats for all those excited little guys.

"Try not to kick up so much dust," Grandpa says with a smile. "This store is cloudier than it was behind the artillery line at the Battle of Yorktown." Grandpa is *way* into American history. He even dresses up sometimes and joins in reenactments of the Revolutionary War.

I try to sweep more carefully, but it's tough. The way people made chocolate three hundred years ago is very different from the way we do it now. Although we try to remove the shells from the cocoa beans neatly, they still get everywhere.

I circle back and carefully sweep out the corners, happy that Mom and Dad told me I could start working here. I mostly like it because I can earn some money, but it's fun to hang out in a working chocolate mill anyway. I put in a few hours each day after school and four or five on the weekend.

The bell over the door jingles and Hannah barges in with Cocoa, Nilla, and Licorice. My sister tosses her backpack on a bench and the dogs start sniffing around.

"When will our dogs understand they're not getting any chocolate?" I say.

"I don't think they ever will. It smells so good!"

I sweep a pile of cocoa shells into my dustpan and dump it into the trash. "Too bad chocolate makes dogs sick," I say. "Could you imagine being around it all the time and not being able to eat a bite?"

Hannah pops a square of plain chocolate into her mouth and smiles. "Nope."

I grab a cloth and start wiping down the

glass pane that visitors look through to see the gears under the mill. Right in the middle, the gear my friend Alan Kunkle and I designed on his 3-D printer smiles at me like a rainbow pinwheel. The mill wouldn't work without it, and it's holding up better than anyone expected.

And none of this would be working without our dogs, which run inside the waterwheel to help get things spinning. They're holding up amazingly well, too!

I move over to the glass case that displays Beatrice Cabot's old cookbook. It sits open to a page where she drew her chocolate-making setup: the heavy chocolate grindstone, her mortar and pestle, and her winnowing basket. A bright red ribbon lies across the page, and I can imagine Great-Great-Great-Great-(however many times)-Grandma Beatrice using it to hold her place in her favorite book.

As I polish the display case, I hear the crunch of gravel in the driveway. A black limousine pulls up.

"I wonder who that could be!" Hannah squeals. "Maybe it's the president! Or better yet, Taylor Swift!"

The driver, a big, burly man in a black hat, gets out. He walks around the car and opens the rear door. A bony man appears. He pushes his floppy brown hair to the side and smooths his jacket.

"Not this jack-a-ninny again," Grandpa mutters.

"Who is it?" I ask, resting on my broom.

His eyes narrow to slits. "The British are coming, Mason. The British are coming."

The man walks along the path that leads to the mill and steps onto the porch.

That's when Cocoa, Nilla, and Licorice pull

free from Hannah's grasp and burst outside. The door swings open and knocks the man back. He tumbles over the railing into a bush. Now all I can see are his legs sticking straight into the air. His pink-and-blue polka-dot socks make me want to laugh.

When he finally crawls out and Grandpa doesn't offer him a hand, I know trouble is brewing.

Chapter 2

"**Mr.** Wentworth, I told you no the first time," Grandpa says.

"Call me Charles," the man says. His accent is definitely English. And with a name like Charles Wentworth, I'm surprised he's not wearing a jeweled crown and holding a scepter.

"Okay, *Charles*, Towne Chocolate Shoppe is not for sale."

"But Mr. Cabot, Regal Candy Corporation is willing to offer—"

"Your offer doesn't matter." Grandpa starts moving the old-fashioned barrels around, something he always does when he's upset. "My name's not even Cabot. That's on the other side of the family. You know nothing about us. You just want to swallow us into your giant company."

The man leans against the counter. "We don't want to swallow you into our giant company," he says. "We want to give you a large sum of money, and *then* swallow you into our giant company. You've done a great job here. You're making chocolates for farmers' markets and reenactments. You're starting to find your way into grocery stores. You have the world's only dog-powered waterwheel. If Regal Candy Corporation takes over, we can bring the price of your chocolate down. That will make your brand available across the country—even worldwide. We're talking millions of dollars."

"I told you we're not interested."

Mr. Wentworth smiles. "In time you'll see it differently."

Grandpa smiles back. "No, we won't."

Mr. Wentworth takes a salted caramel chocolate bar from the rack and fishes a few bills from his wallet. "If you change your mind, I'll be staying at the Quarter Inn Hotel," he says. "Good day."

Mr. Wentworth places the money on the counter and returns to his limousine.

"More like *bad* day," Hannah says. "We're not selling the chocolate mill, are we?"

Grandpa kneels in front of Hannah. "We've worked too hard to get where we are. I'm not about to be pushed around by some fancy suit-wearing aristocrat."

"Aristo-what?" I say.

"An aristocrat is a member of high society," Grandpa says. "Like nobility. In Revolutionary times they'd tootle around in horse-drawn carriages sipping tea. Nowadays, it's stretch limousines and skim soy chai lattes."

I peer out the window as the limousine pulls away. "How much was he offering?"

"The money doesn't matter."

"What if he was offering a million dollars?" I say. "A billion?"

Grandpa hoists a heavy bag of cocoa beans onto his shoulder and starts toward the milling area. "A billion dollars is nothing compared to what we've got."

I look around the mill. Old beams stretch across the ceiling. The waterwheel stands still in the weak stream. "What do we have worth a billion dollars?"

Grandpa turns to me before disappearing downstairs. "We've got plenty."

"Are you hiding a big chest of gold down there behind the grindstone?"

"We've got plenty!" he calls up to me. "Now get those dogs ready. The waterwheel needs to be turning in a few minutes."

I look to Hannah.

She sits on the floor and gathers Cocoa, Nilla, and Licorice around her. Nilla licks at her face. "I think he means we've got each other," she says.

I sit beside Hannah. Licorice jumps on my lap.

"We'd still have each other if we let Regal Candy Corporation give us a big pile of money," I say.

Hannah strokes Nilla's soft back. Nilla drops onto her side and exposes her belly.

"They wouldn't offer us anything unless one of two things was true," Hannah says.

I let Licorice nip onto my sleeve and I tug him around the floor. "What's the first?"

"They're scared of us."

"What would they be scared of?"

Hannah shrugs. "That we could hurt their business somehow or threaten them in some way."

"How could we hurt Regal Candy Corporation? They invented the Choco-Whammy and the Caramel Silk Bar. Regal Candy makes practically every candy bar there is."

Hannah scratches Nilla's belly some more. Our tiny yellow Lab's back leg starts kicking. "Yeah, I don't think that's the reason either."

"Then what's the other possibility?"

Hannah smiles. "Regal Candy knows we're worth way more than a suitcase full of cash."

I smile back and feel a surge of pride. It's been a lot of work to build our company, get the mill turning, and keep it clean every day. Whatever work I've done, Mom, Dad and Grandpa have put in ten times that much. The idea that someone wants to pay us money for it feels good. It means we must be doing something right.

A pained whine comes from the other side of the store.

I look at Hannah.

We both leap up and run around the counter. Cocoa is lying on his side, his legs straight out. He has a worried look on his face. He groans. Around him, chewed wrappers lay scattered about.

"Call Mom and Dad!" Hannah screams. "Call 911!"

"What's the matter?" I ask.

"Cocoa's eaten chocolate. Chocolate is poisonous to dogs!"

www.scholastic.com

www.ellenmiles.net

PUPPLSP11

WHERE EVERY PUPPY FINDS A HOME